HORRiD HENRY'S
Christmas Ambush

HORRiD HENRY'S
Christmas
Ambush

Francesca Simon
Illustrated by Tony Ross

Orion
Children's Books

ORION CHILDREN'S BOOKS

Horrid Henry's Christmas Ambush was first published as *Horrid Henry's Ambush*
and appeared in *Horrid Henry's Christmas Cracker*
First published in Great Britain in 2006
by Orion Children's Books
This edition first published in Great Britain in 2016
by Hodder and Stoughton

1 3 5 7 9 10 8 6 4 2

Text copyright © Francesca Simon, 2006
Illustrations copyright © Tony Ross, 2016

A CIP catalogue record for this book
is available from the British Library.

ISBN 978 1 4440 1608 6

Printed and bound in China

The paper and board used in this book are from well-managed forests
and other responsible sources.

Orion Children's Books
An imprint of
Hachette Children's Group
Part of Hodder and Stoughton
Carmelite House
50 Victoria Embankment
London EC4Y 0DZ

An Hachette UK Company
www.hachette.co.uk
www.horridhenry.co.uk
www.hachettechildrens.co.uk

For Archie, Rufus and Cassian

There are many more
Horrid Henry Early Reader books available.

For a complete list visit:
www.horridhenry.co.uk
or
www.orionchildrensbooks.co.uk

Contents

Chapter 1

It was Christmas Eve at last.
Every minute felt like an hour.
Every hour felt like a year.
How could Henry live until
Christmas morning when he could
get his hands on all his loot?

Mum and Dad were baking
frantically in the kitchen.

Perfect Peter sat by the twinkling
Christmas tree scratching out
'Silent Night' over and over again
on his cello.

"Can't you play something else?"
snapped Henry.

"No," said Peter, sawing away.
"This is the only Christmas carol
I know. You can move if you
don't like it."

"You move," said Henry.

Peter ignored him.

"Siiiiiiiii—lent Niiiiight,"
screeched the cello.

Aaarrrgh.

Horrid Henry lay on the sofa
with his fingers in his ears, double-
checking his choices from the Toy
Heaven catalogue. Big red 'X's
appeared on every page, to help
you-know-who remember all the
toys he absolutely had to have.

Oh please, let everything he
wanted leap from its pages and
into Santa's sack.

After all, what could be better
than looking at a huge glittering stack
of presents on Christmas morning,
and knowing that they were all
for you?

Oh please let this be the year
when he finally got everything
he wanted!

His letter to Father Christmas
couldn't have been clearer.

Dear Father Christmas,
I want loads and loads and
loads of cash, to make up
for the puny amount you put
in my stocking last year.
And a Robomatic Supersonic
Space Howler Deluxe plus
attachments would be great
too. I have asked for this
before, you know!!! And the
Terminator Gladiator fighting
kit. I need lots more Day-
Glo slime and comics and
a Mutant Max poster and
the new Zapatron Hip-Hop
Dinosaur.

This is your last chance.
Henry

P.S. Satsumas are NOT
presents!!!!!
P.P.S. Peter asked me to tell
you to give me all his presents
as he doesn't want any.

How hard could it be for
Father Christmas to get this right?
He'd asked for the Space Howler
last year, and it never arrived.

Instead, Henry got . . . vests.

And handkerchiefs.

And books.

And clothes and a

– blecccch! –

jigsaw puzzle

and a skipping rope

and a tiny Supersoaker
instead of the mega-sized one
he'd specified.

Yuck!

Father Christmas obviously
needed Henry's help.

Father Christmas is getting old
and doddery, thought Henry.
Maybe he hasn't got my letters.
Maybe he's lost his reading glasses.

Or – what a horrible thought –
maybe he was delivering
Henry's presents by mistake
to some other Henry.

Eeeek!

Some yucky, undeserving
Henry was probably right now
this minute playing with Henry's
Terminator Gladiator sword, shield,
axe and trident. And enjoying his
Intergalactic Samurai Gorillas.

It was so unfair!

Then suddenly Henry had a brilliant,
spectacular idea.
Why had he never thought
of this before?
All his present problems would
be over.

Presents were far too important
to leave to Father Christmas.
Since he couldn't be trusted
to bring the right gifts,
Horrid Henry had no choice.

He would have to ambush
Father Christmas.

Chapter 2

Yes!

He'd hold Father Christmas hostage with his Goo-Shooter, while he rummaged in his present sack for all the loot he was owed.

Maybe Henry would keep the lot.
Now *that* would be fair.

Let's see, thought Horrid Henry.
Father Christmas was bound to be
a slippery character, so he'd need to
booby-trap his bedroom.

When you-know-who sneaked in to
fill his stocking at the end of the bed,
Henry could leap up and nab him.

Father Christmas had a lot of
explaining to do for all those years
of stockings filled with satsumas
and walnuts instead of chocolate
and cold hard cash.

So, how best to capture him?
Henry considered.

A bucket of water above the door.

A skipping rope stretched tight across the entrance, guaranteed to trip up intruders.

A web of string criss-crossed from bedpost to door and threaded with bells to ensnare night-time visitors.

And let's not forget strategically scattered whoopee cushions.

His plan was foolproof.
Loot, here I come, thought
Horrid Henry.

Chapter 3

Horrid Henry sat up in bed,
his Goo-Shooter aimed at the
half-open door where a bucket
of water was balanced.
All his traps were laid.

No one was getting in without
Henry knowing about it.
Any minute now, he'd catch Father
Christmas and make him pay up.

Henry waited.
And waited.
And waited.

His eyes started to feel heavy
and he closed them for a moment.

There was a rustling at Henry's door.
Oh my god, this was it!
Henry lay down and pretended
to be asleep.

Cr-eeeek.

Cr-eeeek.

Horrid Henry reached for his
Goo-Shooter.
A huge shape loomed in the
doorway.

Henry braced himself to attack.

"Doesn't he look sweet when he's asleep?" whispered the shape.

"What a little snugglechops," whispered another.

Sweet? Snugglechops?

Horrid Henry's fingers itched
to let Mum and Dad have it
with both barrels.

POW!

SPLAT!

Henry could see it now.
Mum covered in green goo.
Dad covered in green goo.
Mum and Dad snatching the
Goo-Shooter and wrecking all
his plans and throwing out all his
presents and banning him from TV
for ever . . . hmmmn.

His fingers felt a little less itchy.

Henry lowered his Goo-Shooter.
The bucket of water wobbled
above the door.

Yikes!

What if Mum and Dad stepped
into his Santa traps?
All his hard work – ruined.

"I'm awake," snarled Henry.
The shapes stepped back.
The water stopped wobbling.

"Go to sleep!" hissed Mum.
"Go to sleep!" hissed Dad.

"What are you doing here?"
demanded Henry.

"Checking on you," said Mum.
"Now go back to sleep or Father
Christmas will never come."

He'd better, thought Henry.

Chapter 4

Horrid Henry woke with a jolt.
Aaarrggh!
He'd fallen asleep. How could he?

Panting and gasping Henry
switched on the light.
Phew.

His traps were intact.

His stocking was empty.

Father Christmas hadn't been yet.

Wow, that was lucky.
That was incredibly lucky.
Henry lay back, his heart pounding.

And then Horrid Henry had
a terrible thought.

What if Father Christmas had
decided to be spiteful and avoid
Henry's bedroom this year?
Or what if he'd played a
sneaky trick on Henry and filled
a stocking downstairs instead?

Nah. No way.

But wait.
When Father Christmas came to
Rude Ralph's house he always filled
the stockings downstairs.

Now Henry came to think of it,
Moody Margaret always left her
stocking downstairs too, hanging
from the fireplace, not from the end
of her bed, like Henry did.

Horrid Henry looked at the clock.
It was past midnight.
Mum and Dad had forbidden him
to go downstairs till morning,
on pain of having all his presents
taken away and no telly all day.

But this was an emergency.
He'd creep downstairs, take a quick
peek to make sure he hadn't missed
Father Christmas, then be back in
bed in a jiffy.

No one will ever know,
thought Horrid Henry.

Henry tiptoed round the whoopee cushions, leaped over the criss-cross threads, stepped over the skipping rope and carefully squeezed through his door so as not to disturb the bucket of water.

Then he crept downstairs.

Chapter 5

Sneak.

Sneak.

Sneak.

Horrid Henry shone his torch over the sitting room. Father Christmas hadn't been. The room was exactly as he'd left it that evening.

Except for one thing.

Henry's light illuminated the
Christmas tree, heavy with chocolate
santas and chocolate bells and
chocolate reindeer. Mum and Dad
must have hung them on the tree
after he'd gone to bed.

Horrid Henry looked at the
chocolates cluttering up the
Christmas tree.

Shame, thought Horrid Henry, the
way those chocolates spoil the view
of those lovely decorations. You
could barely see the baubles and
tinsel he and Peter had worked so
hard to put on.

"Hi, Henry,"
said the chocolate santas.
"Don't you want to eat us?"

"Go on, Henry,"
said the chocolate bells.
"You know you want to."

"What are you waiting for, Henry?"
urged the chocolate reindeer.

What indeed?
After all, it *was* Christmas.

Henry took a chocolate santa or
three from the side, and then another
two from the back. Hmmn, boy,
was that great chocolate, he thought,
stuffing them into his mouth.

Oops. Now the chocolate santas
looked a little unbalanced.
Better take a few from the front
and from the other side, to even it
up, thought Henry. Then no one
will notice there are a few
chocolates missing.

Henry gobbled and gorged
and guzzled.
Wow, were those chocolates
yummy!!!

Chapter 6

The tree looks a bit bare, thought
Henry a little while later. Mum had
such eagle eyes she might notice that
a few – well, all – of the chocolates
were missing.

He'd better hide all those gaps
with a few extra baubles.

And, while he was improving the tree, he could swap that stupid fairy for Terminator Gladiator.

Henry piled extra decorations onto the branches. Soon the Christmas tree was so covered in baubles and tinsel there was barely a hint of green. No one would notice the missing chocolates.

Then Henry stood on a chair,
dumped the fairy and,
standing on his tippy-tippy toes,
hung Terminator Gladiator
at the top where he belonged.

Perfect, thought Horrid Henry,
jumping off the chair and
stepping back to admire his work.
Absolutely perfect.

Thanks to me
this is the best tree ever.

There was a terrible creaking sound.

Then another.
Then suddenly…

CRASH!

The Christmas tree toppled over.

Horrid Henry's heart stopped.

Upstairs he could hear
Mum and Dad stirring.
"Oy! Who's down there?"
shouted Dad.

RUN!!!
thought Horrid Henry.
Run for your life!!

Horrid Henry ran like he had
never run before, up the stairs to
his room before Mum and Dad
could catch him.

Oh please let him get there in time.

His parents' bedroom door opened
just as Henry dashed inside his room.

He'd made it. He was safe.

SPLASH!

The bucket of water
spilled all over him.

TRIP!

Horrid Henry fell over
the skipping rope.

CRASH!

SMASH!

RING! RING!

jangled the bells.

PLLLLLLL!

belched the whoopee cushions.

"What is going on in here?"
shrieked Mum, glaring.

"Nothing," said Horrid Henry,
as he lay sprawled on the floor
soaking wet and tangled up in
threads and wires and rope.
"I heard a noise downstairs so I got
up to check," he added innocently.

"Tree's fallen over," called Dad. "Must have been overloaded. Don't worry, I'll sort it."

"Get back to bed, Henry," said Mum wearily. "And don't touch your stocking till morning."

Henry looked. And gasped.
His stocking was stuffed
and bulging. That mean old sneak,
thought Horrid Henry indignantly.
How did he do it?
How had he escaped the traps?

Watch out, Father Christmas,
thought Horrid Henry.
I'll get you next year.

What are you going to read next?

Don't miss more Christmas chaos
with Horrid Henry . . .

Watch Henry
steal the show in
**Horrid Henry's
Christmas Play**,

and finally
get his way in
**Horrid Henry's
Christmas
Lunch**.

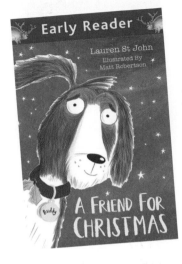

For more festive tales, discover the magic of **A Friend for Christmas**,

or read all about the Nativity story in **The First Christmas**.

Have you read these laugh-out-loud Horrid Henry Early Readers yet?

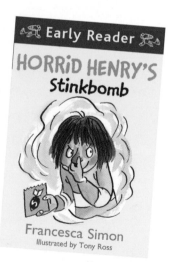